Why I Love My Friends

Illustrated by Daniel Howarth

HarperCollins *Children's Books*

I love my friends because...

we share.

I love my friends because...
they are always there for me.

I love my friends because...

we like the same things.

I love my friends because...
we play hide-and-seek.

I love my friends because...

they are silly.

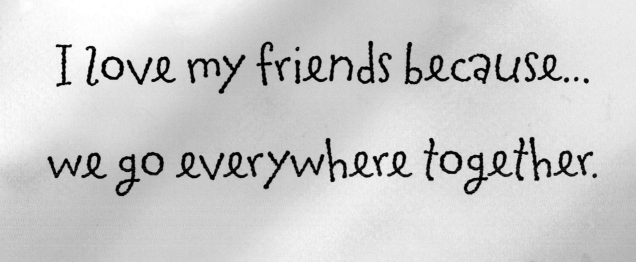

I love my friends because...

we go everywhere together.

I love my friends because...

we hold hands.

I love my
friends because...

we share special moments.

I love my friends
because...

they help me.

I love my
friends because...

we have sleepovers.

Everyone loves their friends,

especially... ME!

First published in hardback in Great Britain by HarperCollins Children's Books in 2016
This edition published in 2019

3 5 7 9 10 8 6 4 2

978-0-00-797703-1

HarperCollins Children's Books is a division of HarperCollins Publishers Ltd.

Text and illustrations copyright © HarperCollins Publishers Ltd 2016

A CIP catalogue record for this title is available from the British Library.
Visit our website at www.harpercollins.co.uk

Printed in China